Too Big!

Geraldine McCaughrean
Illustrated by Peter Bailey

CORGI PUPS

www.booksattransworld.co.uk/childrens

For Joe and Dougie

Series reading consultant: Prue Goodwin
Reading and Language Information Centre,
University of Reading

TOO BIG!
A CORGI PUPS BOOK : 0 552 54618 6

First publication in Great Britain

PRINTING HISTORY
Corgi Pups edition published 1999

5 7 9 10 8 6 4

Set in 18/25pt Bembo Schoolbook by
Phoenix Typesetting, Ilkley, West Yorkshire

Corgi Pups Books are published by Transworld Publishers,
61–63 Uxbridge Road, London W5 5SA,
a division of The Random House Group Ltd,
in Australia by Random House Australia (Pty) Ltd,
20 Alfred Street, Milsons Point, Sydney, NSW 2061, Australia,
and in New Zealand by Random House New Zealand Ltd,
18 Poland Road, Glenfield, Auckland 10, New Zealand
and in South Africa by Random House (Pty) Ltd,
Endulini, 5a Jubilee Road, Parktown 2193, South Africa.

Printed and bound in Great Britain by
Cox & Wyman Ltd, Reading, Berkshire.

CONTENTS

CHAPTER ONE

The Jumper

Dad said the tree in the back garden was too big.

"The roots will damage the house," he said. "The roots take water away from the flowers. It's too big."

But Neil liked the tree. In the mornings its leaves cast a quivering shadow-pattern on his bedroom wall. What is more, it was the ideal tree for a tree-house. Neil had asked and asked to have a tree-house. Mum said, "Perhaps, when you are bigger."

But now that Dad had made up his mind the tree was Too Big, it looked as if the tree would be gone before Neil had time to get any bigger.

It was Saturday. Neil wanted
to swing on the rope tied to a
branch of the big old tree. It
might be his last chance. But
Mum wanted to take him to the
shops.

"I am looking for a new
wardrobe," she said, "and you
need a new jumper."

"Aaah, Mu-u-um!" groaned
Neil.

He did not mean to sound ungrateful, but he and his mother could never agree about clothes.

Other mothers looked for the label in the neck of a shirt, read *6–7 years*, and said: "Ah! This is perfect for my child, who is six (or seven)."

Not Neil's mum. She looked at the label and took out the shirt behind – the one marked *8–9 years*. "You need plenty of room to grow!" she would say.

Unfortunately, Neil never
had time to grow into a shirt
before she bought him another,
two sizes bigger. All Neil's clothes
were too big. They made him
feel like a pea in an egg-cup.

They went to
the shopping
mall and tried
on green
jumpers and
yellow jumpers,
school jumpers
and cricket
jumpers.

"I like this,"
said Neil,
pretending to
bowl a cricket
ball.

"So do I," said his mother. He could hardly believe it! The cricket jumper fitted him perfectly.

"I really, really like this," Neil said, pretending to swing a cricket bat.

"So do I," said Mum. She called the assistant. "We will take this one . . ." she said in her special shopping voice. (Could this really be true? Was she really

going to buy Neil a jumper
which fitted him?) ". . . if you
have it in a bigger size."

Neil did complain a bit, it's true.
"Too big," he said, more than
once. "Too big, *too big*,
toobigtoobigtoobig!" But his
mum only got cross and walked
faster, so that Neil
had to run to
keep up. His
sleeves
flapped
below his
fingertips,

ribbing rippled round his legs.
Soon he had no more breath to
say, "Too big". But he felt like a
satsuma wearing an orange
peel.

Mum led the way to the
furniture store, to look at
wardrobes. She looked at pine
wardrobes and oak wardrobes,

cheap and expensive wardrobes, old, modern and Swedish wardrobes. Sometimes when she opened the door, there was a mirror inside, and Neil saw himself, huge in his jumper. He looked like a cushion in a pillowcase.

"What do you think?" said
his mother.

"Too big," said Neil. Mum
made a cross, gasping noise.

Some of the wardrobes had
mirrors on the *outside*. Big white
ghosts loomed up in the glass,
and all of them were Neil in his
cricket jumper.

"What do you think of this
one?" said his mother.

"Too big," said Neil.

Mum was so cross that she almost stamped. "I'll take this one," she said to the shop assistant, so fiercely that he jumped backwards and fell over a bed.

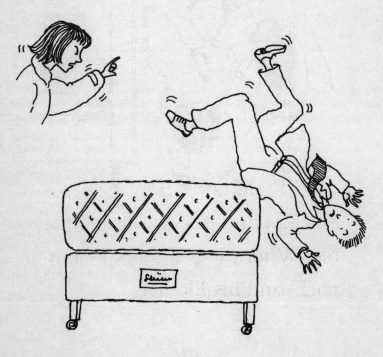

"Too big!
Toobigtoobigtoobig!" said
Neil, until his mother rounded
on him with a pointing finger.

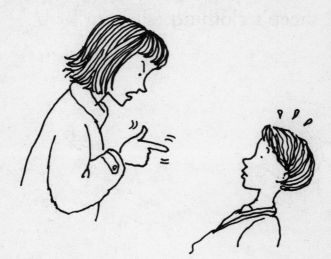

"If you don't stop
complaining about that jumper,
Neil Willis, I shall stop your
pocket money!"

"But I—" The boy in the mirror waved two sorrowful, dangling sleeve-ends in protest.

He looked like a lamb in sheep's clothing.

CHAPTER TWO
The Door

The furniture store delivered the
wardrobe on Friday. It came in
a big van – too big for the
garden gate. So two men had to
carry the wardrobe all the way
up the front path.

Mum saw them coming, opened the front door and went out, smiling.

The men looked at the door, they looked at the wardrobe. "Do you have French windows, missus?" they asked.

"No. Why?"

Well, they turned the wardrobe
on its side,

they turned it
on its end,

they opened the doors and they
took off the door-knobs.

But the wardrobe just *would not* go through the front door. It would not go through the back door either, nor the living-room window.

"I told you at the store," said Neil. "I said it was too big."

His mother glared at him in a quite unreasonable way. And while she glared, and talked about cricket jumpers, the men from the store put down the wardrobe and crept away to their van.

"Stop! You'll have to take it back!" called Mum. But they had already gone.

So when Dad came home, he asked, "Why is there a wardrobe in the front garden?"

Mum explained. (She looked like Neil when he had to explain about breaking the towel rail or losing his school bag. He felt quite sorry for her.) When Dad finished being cross with Mum for buying a wardrobe too big to fit through the door, he said, "I'm sure *I* can get it indoors."

He turned it on its side, he
turned it on its end. He took
off the feet and the door-knobs.

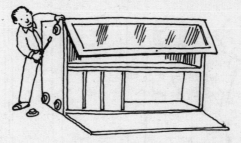

He tried it upside-down and
back to front.

But the front door refused to let
the wardrobe into the house.

"Telephone the store and tell
them to take it back," said Dad.
"It cost too much anyway."

Just as he spoke, it started to rain. The rain drummed on the wardrobe, trickled down the mirror and dripped off the hinges.

"You can't send it back now," said Neil helpfully. "It's too wet."

CHAPTER THREE
The Jitney

Dad had a stroke of genius.

"We can use the window in Neil's room! That's huge! The wardrobe will go through it easily, if we take out the whole window."

"Take out the window?" said his wife doubtfully. "You?"

"I mean I'll ask a carpenter to take out the window. Then we can just haul the wardrobe through!"

"Too big," said Neil. But his parents were busy screwing the knobs back on to the wet wardrobe, and paid no attention.

Mr Bryant down the road was a carpenter. He came along and took out the  window of Neil's room. Dad untied the rope from the 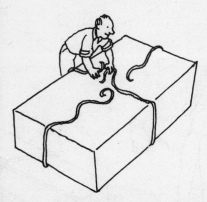 branch of the big old tree and lashed it round the wardrobe. Then he fetched another from the garage, and together he and Mr Bryant stood at Neil's window and pulled.

The wardrobe rocked on its
four corners. The carpenter and
Dad almost pulled themselves
out of the window. But apart
from that, nothing happened.

"Too big," said Neil
unwisely. "I told you
so."

"It is not too big," explained
his father waspishly. "It is
simply too *heavy*."

Neil's dad
was not one to
be defeated
(especially in
front of Mr
Bryant). "We
shall have to

hire a jitney!" he said, pointing
one finger in the air.

"What's a jitney?" asked
Neil.

"Yes, what is a jitney?" asked
Neil's mum.

"A fork-lift truck!" said Mr
Bryant delightedly. "Oh, what
fun!"

"Too big," said Neil, but his parents and Mr Bryant were busy looking in the telephone directory for companies with heavy machinery for hire.

The jitney, when it came, was not too big to fit through the gate. It was a slender, elegant machine painted bright red, with two silver prongs sticking out at the front.

The whole street turned out to watch it trundle down the middle of the road and swing in at Number Fourteen. It rattled up the path and turned left round the side of the house. It had to cross the vegetable patch,

but that could not be helped.

Neil, who was tired of being ignored, sat on the fence and watched. He watched the jitney uproot the carrots and harvest the cabbages. He watched it sink up to its axles, and stop.

The vegetable patch was
damp and newly dug. The jitney
got caught in it like a dinosaur
falling into a tar pit.

All the neighbours came
running to pull it out, but

the driver refused to try again.
He said the jitney would sink
into the back lawn as easily
as into the vegetable patch.

"It's too big, you mean?" said
Neil's dad through gritted teeth.

"Not too big," the driver said, patting his vehicle fondly on her shiny red bumper. "Just too heavy."

CHAPTER FOUR
Now, Everyone

"You could always use the tree," said Neil.

Dad tut-tutted. "We all know how much you like that tree," he said, "but this is no time to be discussing trees."

By now, everyone who lived
in the street stood about in the
garden of Number Fourteen,
discussing how to get a
wardrobe through an upstairs
window.

"What you need is a crane," said Mr Ambrose.

"Too big," said the jitney driver.

"You could leave it where it is and use it for storing your garden tools," suggested Mrs Blenny.

"No, no," said Mum. "It was much too expensive for that!"

"You could make a hole in the wall," suggested Mr Stanley,

 "and carry it up the staircase."

"Too big," said Neil, and Mr Stanley nodded in agreement. The wardrobe would never fit between the banisters.

"Why don't you throw a rope over the top branch of that tree and use it like a pulley?" said Mrs Hogg.

"What a good idea, Mrs Hogg," said Dad.

Neil sank his head into his hands and sighed. Why did no-one ever listen to him?

This was the plan:

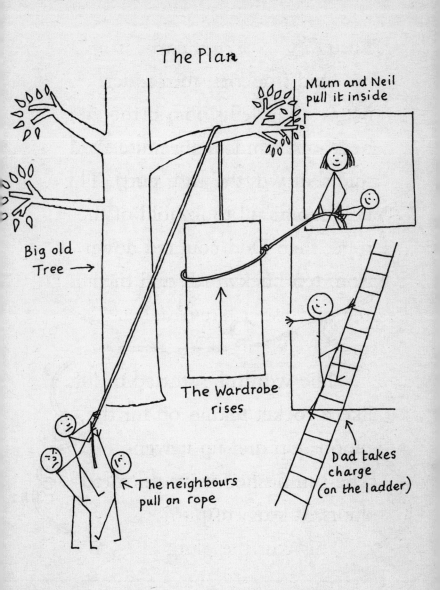

Easy.

Dad stood on the ladder.
Mum and Neil stood in the
bedroom window (because Dad
said that was the easy part). The
neighbours all took hold of the
rope, then Dad counted down
from ten backwards and they
pulled.

The wardrobe started to lift,
like a rocket taking off for the
moon. Up and up it went.
The sun flashed in its mirrored
doors. It was easy.

"This jumper is too big,"
Neil told his mother, as the
wardrobe rose into sight outside.

"Not now, Neil," Mum said,
pulling on the rope to swing the
wardrobe in over the sill. "The
curtains are catching. Just hold
the rope while I free them . . ."

Neil tried. He really did. He made a grab for the rope, but the sleeves of his new cricket jumper were dangling down over his fingers, and he just could not get a grip.

The rope slipped through his white woollen cuffs, and the wardrobe swung out and away from the house, like Tarzan on a jungle creeper.

It knocked over the ladder
with Dad on it, and crashed up
against the tree, wedging itself
between two branches.

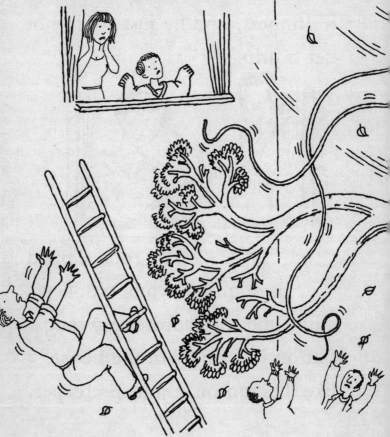

The neighbours were so
scared by the loud noise that
they let go of their rope.

Neil poked his head out of the window and flapped his sleeve-ends.

"Sorry!" he called. "My jumper was too big, you see!"

CHAPTER FiVE
Just Right

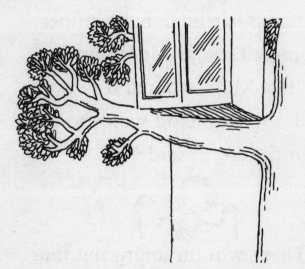

Mrs Blenny looked up at the wardrobe in the tree. "Just right," she said.

Mr Stanley agreed. "Just right."

"I always wanted one when I was a lad," said the jitney-driver.

"Couldn't have built a finer one myself," said Mr Bryant.

"But Mum wanted a new wardrobe, and Dad wants to cut down the tree," said Neil.

There was an angry murmur among the neighbours.

"Cut down the tree?" said Mr Ambrose. "But we can see that tree from all over. It's a fine old tree!"

"A person can't just *cut down* a tree!" said Mrs Hogg hotly. "There are laws!"

"No, no. Of course not," said Dad, turning an odd shade of pink.

"It's a local landmark," Mr Ambrose insisted.

"Yes, yes. Of course it is," said Dad.

"Especially with a tree-house in it," said the jitney-driver.

It was true: the wardrobe made
a wonderful tree-house. The
ladder just reached to it. The
inside was big enough for a boy,
while the shelves on one side

held plenty of books and toys,
and secret things like telescopes
and signal flags and pieces of
rope.

That summer holiday, Neil spent all his time going up and down the ladder. The weather was warm. He wore T-shirts and shorts. They were still one or two sizes too big, but Neil did not care.

His tree-house was just the right size.

THE END!